Annika Mae's House

Hen and Chicks' Marsh

Mole's Hole

Y0-CAG-033

Our Friend Hedgehog

THE STORY OF US

Lauren Castillo

Our Friend Hedgehog

THE STORY OF US

DANVILLE PUBLIC LIBRARY
DANVILLE, INDIANA

Alfred A. Knopf

New York

THIS IS A BORZOI BOOK PUBLISHED BY ALFRED A. KNOPF

This is a work of fiction. Names, characters, places, and incidents either are the product of the author's imagination or are used fictitiously. Any resemblance to actual persons, living or dead, events, or locales is entirely coincidental.

Copyright © 2020 by Lauren Castillo

All rights reserved. Published in the United States by Alfred A. Knopf, an imprint of Random House Children's Books, a division of Penguin Random House LLC, New York. Knopf, Borzoi Books, and the colophon are registered trademarks of Penguin Random House LLC.

Visit us on the Web! rhcbooks.com

Educators and librarians, for a variety of teaching tools, visit us at RHTeachersLibrarians.com

Library of Congress Cataloging-in-Publication Data is available upon request.

ISBN 978-1-5247-6671-9 (trade) — ISBN 978-1-5247-6672-6 (lib. bdg.) — ISBN 978-1-5247-6673-3 (ebook)

The illustrations in this book were created using pen, pencils, watercolor, and Photoshop. Book design by Martha Rago

MANUFACTURED IN CHINA
May 2020
10 9 8 7 6 5 4 3 2 1

First Edition

Random House Children's Books supports the First Amendment and celebrates the right to read.

For every friend (and furry friend) I have had,
and will have, in this lifetime: Thank you
for being a part of my story.

CONTENTS

the Cast

Annika Mae
Flores

Beaver

Hedgehog

Mutty

Owl

Mole

Hen and
Chicks

Our Friend
Hedgehog

THE STORY OF US

Introduction

Sometimes you make a friend and it feels like you have known that friend your entire life. Hedgehog, Mutty, Mole, Owl, Beaver, Hen and Chicks, and me, Annika Mae.

You might think it has always been this way, but it has not.

There was a series of events that brought us all together.

This is our friendship story.

This is the story of us.

at first

Between the great forests, in the center of
the river, on a teeny-tiny island, lived two
dear friends: Hedgehog and Mutty.

Just the two of them, and no one else.

They spent all their days together.

Playing.

Imagining.

Dreaming.

There were moments when the island felt
lonely and Hedgehog wished for more.

But most of the time, she was just happy to
be with her friend.

Life was good.

That was, until the night of the Terrible
Storm. A storm that brought the meanest
wind Hedgehog had ever known.

It whistled.

It huffed.

It swooped down

and carried her friend away.

alone

Hedgehog was all alone. She called out for Mutty, again and again, but only the mean wind answered.

Hedgehog sat and wept. And wept. And wept some more. But crying would not

bring Mutty back. She knew what she
needed to do.

Hedgehog stood up. She stared long and
hard at her reflection in the murky river
water.

She took a deep breath, jumped in, and set off on a journey to find her dear friend.

The river was rough, but luckily Hedgehog was a good swimmer. She could swim all the strokes, including the backstroke (which was her favorite).

Hedgehog made it safely to the mainland,
where the forest began. She had watched the
wind carry Mutty in this direction, and she
hoped she would find him here, safe among
the trees.

Hedgehog had seen the forest from her island, but it was even greater and *much* more frightening now that she was standing in it. An army of trees blew and swayed, and cast their scary shadows over her. But she would not show her fear.

Hedgehog stood up tall and marched along, calling Mutty's name whenever she heard a sound. She marched and marched, called and called again. Not a Mutty in sight. In this big, foreign place, Hedgehog felt smaller than ever before.

She missed her tiny island, but she had to keep going. She searched under ferns and in clusters of mushrooms. Then she climbed onto a stump to get a better view.

Most things in the forest reminded
Hedgehog of her friend, but a passing
butterfly made her saddest of all.

It was beginning to get dark, and still there
was no sign of Mutty. Hedgehog scouted
out a safe place to rest
until she could
continue her
search in the
morning.

She had just
found a nice,
cozy pile of
leaves, when

down,

down,

down

into a hole she plunged!

Splash!

Hedgehog landed in a big puddle of muck. When her eyes adjusted to the dark, she realized she was not alone.

"Good heavens!" shrieked a voice.

A *stranger*! Hedgehog gasped and shot up out of the mud. She was standing face to face with the most wiggly creature she had ever seen.

"Wh-who are you?"

"Oh! Bonjour, dearie," said the voice. "Hello there. My name is Mole. Welcome to my home."

Mole wiggled closer to Hedgehog.

"Are you okay? Are you lost?"

Hedgehog tried to respond, but Mole's bright apron captured her attention. The stripy pattern blurred in Hedgehog's teary eyes, and she collapsed into a puddle of

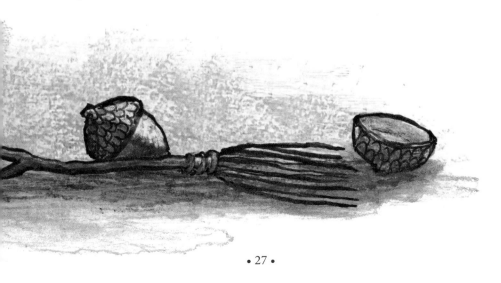

sadness. She was too sad to even speak.

"There, there, my dearie. It will be okay."

Hedgehog looked up at Mole. "I–I lost my best friend," she whimpered.

"I am sorry." Mole patted Hedgehog on the back. "I will help you find your friend." Mole brought Hedgehog a cup of horchata, her favorite milky drink, and the two sat side by side in silence.

After a while, Hedgehog was ready to tell Mole what had happened to poor Mutty. About the whistling wind and her long, hard journey traveling across the river and through the trees.

"I have never, ever been without Mutty, and he has never been without me,"

Hedgehog explained. "We need each other."

Mole was a *very* good listener. She nodded in all the right places and rested a comforting paw on Hedgehog's quills. It felt good to have someone to talk to in this big, scary forest.

"Thank you, Mole," Hedgehog sighed. "I am glad I fell into your home."

"I'm glad you stopped by," said Mole. "I love visitors. I'm only sorry my home is such a mess. It's more like a rat's nest than a mole's hole ever since the storm. I was just tidying up when you arrived."

Mole wiggled backward, knocking over an acorn cap that was collecting tiny drips of water from the ceiling.

"Here, let me help you," offered Hedgehog. The two sopped up the puddles together, and soon Mole's home was as good as new.

"I have come up with a plan, dearie," announced Mole.

"I will take you to Owl at Lookout Point.
Owl has sharp eyes, and he can help us find
your friend. We should travel by tunnel. It's
the safest route."

Hedgehog was nervous about traveling
in a tunnel. But she trusted her new friend.
"Lead the way, Mole." And Hedgehog
followed wiggly Mole through the tunnel

toward the other side of the forest.

"You are brave to travel so far from home!"
Hedgehog shouted up to Mole.

"Oh, I love to travel!" said Mole. "But
sometimes it's lonely underground. It is
very nice to have company."

Hedgehog still missed poor Mutty, but
this adventure with Mole brought her a
bit of cheer. "It *is* nice to have company,"
she agreed.

owl

When Mole and Hedgehog arrived at
Lookout Point, it was nearly daybreak. The
tired pair wiggled out of Mole's tunnel and
right into a patch of fog. But the fog was no
match for Owl's sharp eyes.

"Hooty hoot, who goes there?" called Owl. Owl never missed a trick.

"Guten Tag, Owl! Good day," said Mole. "This is my new friend, Hedgehog. She needs our help."

"Help?" Owl perked up. "What kind of help?"

"I lost my best friend, in the . . ." Hedgehog trailed off, beginning to weep again.

"Foggy weather is terrible for hide-and-seek, my little hoglet."

Mole spoke up for Hedgehog. "We are not playing hide-and-seek, Owl. We are talking about a friend in *peril.*"

"Hmm, peril?" Owl pondered. "You mean *very serious and immediate danger.* Well, I *do* happen to have fast wings and excellent eyes. Maybe I *can* help! Which way did your friend go?"

"I–I don't know," Hedgehog sobbed.

Mole put her arm around Hedgehog and told Owl all about what had happened to Mutty.

"What does your friend look like?" asked Owl. He pulled out a pen and notebook, ready to take notes.

"I can draw him," said Hedgehog.

Hedgehog borrowed Owl's pen and notebook. Most of the pages were full of

cheerful-looking pictures and words, but
she found a blank page toward the back
and carefully sketched a portrait of Mutty.
Hedgehog liked to draw in the sand on her
island, so she was pretty good at it.

"This drawing is in black, but he wears
red and white and gray and orange,"
Hedgehog explained.

"Well, look at that," said Owl as he examined the drawing. "Finding him will be a true challenge in this weather. But I'm up for it!"

"Oh, thank you," said Hedgehog. "Thank you, Owl."

"Let me gather my ideas," said Owl. And he flew into the foggy sky, making circles around Lookout Point and humming an idea-gathering tune.

"I've got it!" Owl exclaimed. "We will follow the stream to the beaver dam. All kinds of things get trapped in that dam. Maybe the storm has taken your friend there."

"Good idea, Owl!" cheered Mole.

"I know," said Owl, beginning to fly upstream. "I'll meet you two at the beaver dam. . . ."

Mole and Hedgehog jumped into the tunnel and sped after him, practically flying underground.

Beaver

By the time Mole and Hedgehog emerged from the tunnel, the fog was beginning to clear. Owl was telling Beaver about their quest to find Mutty. Beaver was busy rebuilding his dam, though, and he didn't seem very interested.

"Wretched storm ruined my masterpiece," Beaver grumbled.

"Beaver!" cried Owl. "I am trying to show you something!" He waved the notebook in Beaver's face. "Have you seen this fella? Have you noticed anything out of the ordinary that might help us find him?"

"Nope, nope," said Beaver as he reached for a piece of red fabric.

"Mutty!" shrieked Hedgehog.

"Where?!" Owl and Mole jumped.

"It's Mutty's scarf!" Hedgehog pointed at the red scarf, which Beaver was now tying neatly about his neck.

"Huh? Nope, nope!" Beaver waved them

off. "This is *my* scarf. I found it, and now it's mine!"

"Beaver!" cried Owl. "You *just* said you hadn't seen anything out of the ordinary!"

"Well, I forgot," huffed Beaver. "Now leave me alone."

"We are not going anywhere without that scarf!" screeched Owl.

"Well, I'm not taking it off," Beaver grumbled. "My neck is cold. . . . And plus, look how dapper I am." He fluffed up his fur and adjusted the scarf just so.

Owl got right in Beaver's face. "You have two choices, Beaver. Either give us that scarf or come help us."

Beaver snorted. "I don't have to do *either* of those things."

Owl narrowed his eyes.

"I will come along . . . but only 'cause I feel like it. Not 'cause you said," Beaver added quickly.

"Thank you, Beaver," said Hedgehog. "And you *do* look dapper in Mutty's scarf."

Beaver looked away, a blush rising to his chubby cheeks. "Like I said."

"Dapper." Owl looked Beaver up and down. *"Neat and trim in appearance."*

"Now, where did you find the scarf?" asked Hedgehog.

"Over at the marsh, near Hen's house, when I was—"

"Then *that's* where we'll go next," Owl interrupted. "Let's get moving!"

Beaver
examined
the ground.
"It's too muddy
to walk. We'll
have to take my
raft."

Hedgehog looked at Mole,
who was wiggling more than usual.

"It's okay, Mole. Hold my paw."

"But I'm afraid of the water," Mole
whispered. "Can't we take the tunnel?"
"If you fall in, I promise to save you. I'm a
good swimmer."

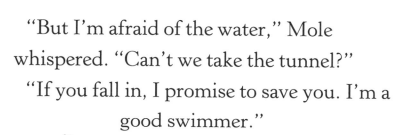

And the whole crew piled onto
Beaver's raft.

The water was still very
choppy from the storm, and the

raft rocked this way and that.

Poor Mole clung to the boards, wiggling with fear.

"Holy Toledo!" she cried. "Of all my voyages, this one might be the scariest yet!"

"Slow down, Beaver," Hedgehog pleaded. "Not everyone can swim!"

At that moment, Beaver steered right into a rock, knocking Mole and Hedgehog into the stream! The current whipped them about, but Hedgehog was able to keep Mole's snout above water.

Beaver held out his paddle. "Grab on!"

he called. They did as they were told, and
Beaver pulled them aboard.

"You'd better be more careful, Beaver!"
Owl screeched.

"Everyone is back on the raft, aren't
they?" said Beaver.

For the rest of the ride, Hedgehog held on
to poor shivery Mole. This time patting *her*
on the back.

HEN and Chicks

Beaver rowed up to the edge of the marsh and helped his passengers out, one by one.

"I found the red scarf right there." Beaver pointed.

The marsh was littered with all kinds of

trash that the wind had blown in during
the Terrible Storm. There were bottles and
cans, a pizza box with some uneaten crust,
a rotten apple core, some playing cards, and
plenty of other curious objects.

"Everyone spread out, and we'll search the
wetland for Hedgehog's friend," called Owl.

The crew did as Owl said. They looked under branches, in bushes, around the tall marsh grass.

They found a snapping turtle,

three slimy snails,

and a school of small fish,

but no Mutty.

"Peep! Peep! Peep!" Two peeping chicks bounced out of the brush and caught Hedgehog by surprise.

Chick One bounced off Beaver's tail. Chick Two followed right behind.

"Ow!" Beaver grunted.

"¡Hola! Hello, lively little Chicks," Mole said with a smile.

"Chicks!" called Owl. "Chicks, where is your mom? We have a very important matter to discuss with her."

"Peep!" Chick Two bounced off Chick One. "Peep, peep!" Chick One bounced off Chick Two. And the two leap-chicked right back into the brush.

"For peep's sake!" groaned Beaver.

"Let's follow them," said Mole. "I'm sure Hen is close by."

They followed the peeps through the brush. On the other side they

found Hen,
pecking through the
storm trash.

"Salaam, Hen," called Mole.

"Oh, hello, Mole! Hello,
Beaver and Owl!" Hen looked at
Hedgehog. "And um . . . hello,
pointy creature I don't know. I'm
out collecting storm treasure.

Would you look at this." Hen balanced a piece of treasure on her head. "A crown!"

"Nope, nope. That's a bottle top," said Beaver.

Hen ignored him. "And how about this one? Pirate's booty! And new art for the chicks' room!"

Hedgehog's eyes widened. It was a picture of a house. But in front of the house was a familiar face.

"Mutty!" she shrieked.

"What is it this time?" asked Owl.

"Th-the picture!" Hedgehog stuttered. "Mutty is in the picture."

"Our new friend Hedgehog lost her old friend Mutty," Mole explained to Hen, who was looking confused.

"But how did your friend get in my art?" asked Hen.

"It's a photograph," Owl said. *"A picture made using a camera."*

"Who took the picture?" asked Hedgehog.

"I think that's what we're all wondering!" Owl said.

"Well, I don't know who took the picture . . . but I *do* know this house." Hen pointed.

"You–you do?" Hedgehog perked up.

"Yes indeed. I can take you there if you like."

"Oh, yes please!" cried Hedgehog.

"Wonderful!" whooped Owl.

"How terrific!" cheered Mole.

"How far is it?" grumbled Beaver.

"It's through the marsh, at the top of Tall Hill. I think a new family just moved in,"

Hen announced. "I can show you, but will you help carry my treasures?"

"Sure," said Owl. "Just be careful with the notebook."

"What notebook?" Hen wondered aloud
as she stowed her booty in Owl's empty bag.
But the others were already marching
toward Tall Hill, and the notebook was
soon forgotten.

ANNika Mae Flores

Annika Mae was photographing her new
backyard when she saw the parade of
animals approaching. There was a hen,
two chicks, a beaver, an owl, a mole, and a
hedgehog. And they were headed toward

her house! She hadn't had any visitors since the move. She snapped a quick photo, then ran down Tall Hill to greet them.

"Hello!" Annika Mae called.

"Hooty hoot, hello!" Owl called back.

"My name is Annika Mae. What are your names?"

"I am Owl," said Owl. "This here is Hen, and those are her chicks peeping about. Over there is Mole, wiggling next to Hedgehog."

"Anyoung! Hello there!" Mole waved.

"Oh, and Beaver is back by the rock, preening, or *devoting effort to making oneself look attractive.*"

"We are hoping you can help us with something, por favor," Mole said, tugging the art treasure out of Owl's bag.

"My Polaroid!" Annika Mae exclaimed.

"Po-Po-Polaroid?" stuttered Hedgehog. "His name isn't Polaroid. It's Mutty."

"Oh. No, I mean the picture is called a Polaroid. It was taken with my Polaroid camera." Annika Mae held up the camera around her neck and snapped a quick shot of Hedgehog.

"See?" She placed a new Polaroid on the ground. All the animals gathered round to watch as a picture of Hedgehog magically appeared.

"This is your Polaroid?" Hedgehog was confused. "Then maybe you know

where the dog in the picture is?"

"Is that *your* dog?" asked Annika Mae.
"Maybe you could describe him a little
more. Does he have the softest fuzz you
ever felt?"

"Yes . . . ," said Hedgehog.

"Does he have eyes the color of midnight?"

"Yes . . ."

"And a chocolate-brown stitched nose?"

"Yesss."

Annika Mae grinned as she reached into her overalls pocket. "Is it *this* dog?"

"Mutty!" Hedgehog screamed with glee.

Hedgehog gave her best friend the biggest hug in the whole wide world.

She could tell Mutty had missed her, too.

"I found him at the edge of the stream last night," said Annika Mae. "He was all covered in mud, so I carried him home and cleaned him up. It was nice having company in that big house."

Hedgehog knew Mutty was the best company. She couldn't stop smiling as she held Mutty's soft, clean paws in hers.

"Thank you for rescuing my
best friend, Annika Mae."

"You're welcome, little Hedgehog.
I hope you don't mind if I keep this Polaroid.
It must have fallen out of my knapsack
when I was searching for my notebook."

"Of course," Hen said. "I collected other
treasures today."

"Did you ever find your notebook?" asked
Hedgehog.

"No," sighed Annika Mae. "I left it out in
the yard before the storm yesterday, and I
think it may be gone for good. It was filled
with stories I wrote about my old home with
my friends Josie and Mateo. They live very
far away now. Almost six hours by plane."

Hedgehog heard the sadness in Annika Mae's voice and hugged Mutty to her chest. "I'll help you look for your notebook, Annika Mae," said Hedgehog.

"We are very good at finding important things, dearie," said Mole, standing up tall. "Now, what does the notebook look like?"

"Thank you." Annika Mae smiled. "It's bright red, with words and pictures inside."

Hedgehog and Mole looked at Owl, who was unusually quiet.

"Hmm, that sounds like *your* notebook, Owl," said Beaver.

"Oh," Owl said. "Well, I do have an awful lot of books. I must have picked it up, thinking it was one of mine."

"You found my notebook?!" Annika Mae jumped up and down.

"Well, I *did* find it . . ." Owl was emptying his bag now. There was Hen's pirate's booty, and Owl's pen, and not a thing more. "But it seems to be lost again," he finished.

"Nope, nope," grumbled
Beaver. "It is right where
you left it, on top of my dam!"

"I'll go get your notebook,
Annika Mae!" announced
Hedgehog. She could picture
exactly where Owl had set it down.
"You saved my best friend, and now
I want to save your notebook."

"Don't be silly," said Owl. "You can't fly there like I can. *I* will get the notebook."

Hedgehog puffed her quills. "I can't fly, but I can swim." She sat Mutty down next to Annika Mae. "You stay here with your new friends, Mutty. I will be back soon." And Hedgehog took off toward the stream.

THE NOTEBOOK

Hedgehog swam swiftly upstream. As she approached the dam, she spotted the notebook, exactly where Beaver had said it would be. She climbed up the newly built dam, stepping carefully on one shifting

branch and then the next until she got to
the top.

Hedgehog reached for the notebook, but it
didn't budge. She tugged harder. Still stuck.

She grabbed the notebook with both paws,
leaned back, and tugged with all her
hedgehoggy might.

Whoosh!

The notebook went flying through the air, and in the same instant there came a terrible groan as the dam collapsed beneath Hedgehog's feet!

Splash! Crash!

All of Beaver's carefully chosen branches went tumbling downstream, along with Hedgehog and the now very soggy notebook.

Hedgehog fought to keep herself above the rapids, bobbing up and down like a buoy. Every time she got close to the notebook, the water pulled her under and she lost sight of it again.

"HELP! HELP!" Hedgehog cried out, but water rushed into her mouth, and the sound that came out was more like "Hoggglle! Hoooggggle!"

As the rough waters carried her away, she had a dreadful thought: What if she drifted so far that she couldn't find her way back? What if she never saw Mutty again? And what about Mole, and Beaver, and Owl? Hen and Chicks, and Annika Mae?! She had only just met them, but it was horrible to imagine a life without them! Was this how Annika Mae had felt when she moved away from her old friends?

"Calamity!" She heard a familiar screech from far away. "Calamity, Annika Mae! *A disaster!*"

It was Owl–she was not alone!

That thought gave Hedgehog a boost of super-hedgehoggy strength. She didn't know if she could rescue the notebook . . . but she wasn't going to lose her friends!

Hedgehog saw a large rock in the middle of the stream. If she could guide herself to

it, maybe she could get
her quills above water.
She reached for a thick piece
of bark and used it as a kickboard,
flutter-kicking her hind legs as fast as she
could. With the last of her strength, she
lunged forward onto the rock.

"Little Hedgehoooog! Little Hedgehog,
we're coming for yooouuu! DON'T LET
GO OF THAT ROCK!"

Hedgehog shifted her weight to get a better grip, and her paw landed on the red notebook—somehow it had washed up right beside her!

Annika Mae was swimming toward Hedgehog with determined strokes. Hedgehog reached for the notebook to hand it to Annika Mae, but without hesitating, Annika Mae scooped up Hedgehog instead. Beaver popped up behind her and grabbed the notebook. Together, the three of them waded to the riverbank, Hedgehog safely tucked in Annika Mae's arms.

Mole, Mutty, and Hen and Chicks
watched in suspense. Owl circled overhead.
"Hurrah!" cheered the friends when
Annika Mae, Hedgehog, and Beaver

returned to shore. And everyone piled into one big hug.

"You scared us, Hedgehog!" Owl screeched.

Annika Mae dropped to the ground with relief. "Phewie, little Hedgehog!"

"Great grasshoppers! You had us worried," said Mole.

"Yes! Peep! Peep! Peep!" Hen and Chicks chimed in.

"Hey, what about my dam?" griped Beaver.

"Beaver!" scolded Owl.

"I mean, I'm glad you didn't drown," Beaver mumbled.

Hedgehog grinned. She was lucky to have such brave friends.

Hedgehog walked over to the red notebook drying in the sun in Annika Mae's backyard. It wasn't looking so great. The pages were dirty. And some were torn. The writing was faded and smudged. What a mess.

She looked up at Annika Mae, who was wiping a tear from her eye. "I'm sorry, Annika Mae," Hedgehog said with an unsteady voice. "I ruined your notebook."

"Don't be silly. You didn't ruin my notebook, Hedgehog."

"Yes, I did. If I hadn't tried to pull it out of the dam, none of this would have happened."

"Hedgehog, you were very brave to try and save my notebook. You put yourself at risk. I'm just glad *you're* okay."

Hedgehog flipped through the red notebook again. The writing was faded, but maybe she could trace over the letters. The pages were torn, but maybe she could tape them back together.

"Maybe we can fix it . . . ," she said.

"We could try," said Annika Mae.

She disappeared into the house, and when she returned, she was carrying a big bag of art supplies. There were a hundred

different colors of markers, tiny tubes of brightly colored paint, pawfuls of crayons and colored pencils, small brushes and big ones, jars of glitter, scissors and glue, and more tools still that none of them could name.

"Peep! Peep! Peep!" The chicks started poking their beaks into the pile and took off with a couple of crayons.

"Come back here, naughty Chicks!" clucked Hen. And she went chasing after them.

Beaver couldn't contain himself, either.

He had already built a tiny house out of
Popsicle sticks and was now tangled up in
three colors of ribbon, for some reason.

Hedgehog grabbed an inky blue pen from
the pile. "I bet you are a very
good writer, Annika
Mae," she said,
starting to
trace the
letters. She
couldn't read
them, but she
knew how to
follow the lines.

"Thank you," said Annika Mae. "But I
didn't write these stories on my own—

I wrote them with the help of my old friends. We had great adventures together."

Hedgehog closed her eyes and thought about all that she had been through with Mutty.

"Hmmm," said Mole, pulling her snout out of a jar of glitter. "Maybe you could write some *new* stories with your *new* friends, dearie."

"My *new* friends . . ." Annika Mae smiled.
"I like the sound of that."

Hedgehog looked around the backyard.
At Mutty, Mole, Owl, Beaver, Hen and
Chicks, and Annika Mae. She could feel her
heart expanding in her chest.

"So do I," Hedgehog said. Then she
opened the notebook to a blank page and
handed it to Annika Mae.

"What are we waiting for?"

Hedge Hollow

Beaver's Dam

Owl's Lookout

Hedgehog's Island

DANVILLE PUBLIC LIBRARY
DANVILLE INDIANA